SHORT TALES
Fables

The **TORTOISE** and the **HARE**

Adapted by Shannon Eric Denton
Illustrated by Mark Pennington

magic wagon

visit us at www.abdopublishing.com

Published by Magic Wagon, a division of the ABDO Group, 8000 West 78th Street, Edina, Minnesota, 55439. Copyright © 2010 by Abdo Consulting Group, Inc. International copyrights reserved in all countries. All rights reserved. No part of this book may be reproduced in any form without written permission from the publisher.

Short Tales ™ is a trademark and logo of Magic Wagon.

Printed in the United States of America, North Mankato, Minnesota.
092009
012010

Adapted Text by Shannon Eric Denton
Illustrations by Mark Pennington
Colors by Robby Bevard
Edited by Stephanie Hedlund
Interior Layout by Kristen Fitzner Denton
Book Design and Packaging by Shannon Eric Denton

Library of Congress Cataloging-in-Publication Data

Denton, Shannon Eric.
  The tortoise and the hare / adapted by Shannon Eric Denton ; illustrated by Mark Pennington.
     p. cm. -- (Short tales. Fables)
  ISBN 978-1-60270-555-5
  [1. Fables. 2. Folklore.] I. Pennington, Mark, 1959- ill. II. Aesop. III. Title.
  PZ8.2.D34To 2010
  398.2--dc22
  [E]
                          2008032323

One sunny day, a hare sat by a tree.

The hare watched a tortoise approach.

The tortoise was slow.

The hare laughed at the slow tortoise.

"You're the slowest thing I've ever seen!" the hare said.

"You shouldn't make fun of me," said the tortoise.

"There is nothing you can do about it," the hare said.

"That's not true," said the tortoise.

"Do you want to race?" asked the tortoise. The hare couldn't stop laughing.

The hare agreed, and soon they were racing.

The hare ran very far ahead of the tortoise.

"You'll never catch me," laughed the hare.

The hare grew tired and decided to take a nap.

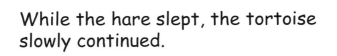

While the hare slept, the tortoise slowly continued.

When the hare woke up, the tortoise was crossing the finish line!

The moral of the story is:

Slow and steady wins the race!